Emily Alston

When You Can't See Me Smile

EXPRESSING AND UNDERSTANDING
FEELINGS AND EMOTIONS
WHILE WEARING A MASK

I'm wearing a mask on my way to school,

And I am feeling okay
and feeling cool.

But a little **worry**
is buzzing
in my head.

How will my friends know if I'm **happy**,

or **sad** instead?

THEY CAN'T SEE MY SMILE
BEHIND MY MASK!

I WONDER IF THEY'LL THINK TO ASK?

How will they know
when I feel **surprised**

that Suzy and I have got the same ride?

How will they know
that I'm **anxiously** waiting,
to be the next one to go up presenting?

How will they know that

I'M SO EXCITED,

CHEERFUL,
AND HOPEFUL,
AND SIMPLY
DELIGHTED...

...to have lunch together again
as a group.

(With new rules in place, of course, and that's good.)

WORST OF ALL,
HOW WILL I KNOW

HOW THEY FEEL?

I'm a little **confused**,
and the worry is real!

But I can **hear** Suzy laughing out loud.

And I **notice** Tom yelling all excited and proud.

And **I see** Jake
standing nearby,
being quiet
and a little bit
shy.

So I can use **words** and my **voice** to express,
if I'm feeing okay or I'm feeling distress.

And I can **listen** for the words of others,
that tell me if they're frustrated (with math)
or just mad at their brothers.

And I can **see** expressions and gestures with my eyes,
and know how others are feeling without a surprise.

And I can **show** my friends just how I feel
without using words or making a squeal,
by using **non-verbal** actions and behaviors,
like waving my hand or doing some favors.

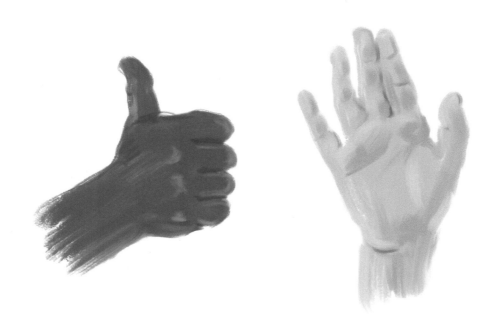

WHEN I CAN'T SEE CLEARLY
THE EMOTIONS IN OTHERS,

I NEED TO USE CLUES
TO SEARCH AND DISCOVER,
HOW OTHERS ARE FEELING.

So when we're wearing masks,
I'll be on the hunt for

WORDS,

GESTURES,

and

EYES,

EYEBROWS,
HALF-FACE EXPRESSIONS,

and

SMILES in disguise.

I'll be looking for clues, and cues, and other traces
of feelings and emotions
on **half-hidden faces**.

And I'll also make sure to find creative ways
to show my friends just how I'm feeling,
even when my mask is concealing...

MY SMILE.

BECAUSE,
COMMUNICATION MAKES
A SOLID FOUNDATION
FOR GOOD RELATIONS
WITH MY FRIENDS.

AND KNOWING HOW MY FRIENDS
ARE DOING
IS ALWAYS THE BEST.

CPSIA information can be obtained
at www.ICGtesting.com
Printed in the USA
LVHW071802130321
681466LV00002B/61